Stemmer House ™

Inquiries should be directed to
Stemmer House Publishers, Inc.
2627 Caves Road
Owings Mills, Maryland 21117

*A Barbara Holdridge book*

Printed in Great Britain and bound in the United States of America

First American Edition

**Library of Congress Cataloging in Publication Data**
Williams, Leslie, 1941–
    A bear in the air.
    SUMMARY: A small boy spends the day with a fantasy-
bear whom he discovers among the clouds in the sky.
    [1. Bears—Fiction. 2. Fantasy] I. Vendrell,
Carme Solé, 1944–   II. Title.
PZ7.W6667Be 1980     [E]          80–10290
ISBN 0–916144–54–2

# A Bear in the Air

Story by
Leslie Williams

Pictures by
Carme Solé Vendrell

1980

Stemmer
House
PUBLISHERS, INC.

Owings Mills, Maryland

Have you ever spent a summer afternoon watching the clouds tumble through the sky? Then you will know how this story begins. But if you have never stretched out on the warm grass and looked up to see the passing clouds, then first I should tell you that clouds are full of faces and animals and whatever you will.

One summer afternoon, when big white clouds were tumbling through the sky, a boy lay on his back in the warm grass to watch the passing figures overhead.

So far he had seen two very big dragons and a rhinoceros that had floated over him and drifted off towards the sea. Now, just coming over the hill, there was something round and promising—perhaps an ear. Then a muzzle appeared and two fluffy white paws.

"There's a bear in the air," said the boy to himself. He so liked the sound of this that he said it again, out loud. "There's a bear in the air."

Then, over the side of the hill, came something which looked like a very large and comfortable cave.

"There's a lair for the bear," thought the boy. Suddenly there was a sound like a distant rumble of thunder. The boy sat up. Had the bear said something? The bear rumbled again. It was an unhappy kind of growl.

"You there!" said the bear. The boy looked around. The bear must mean him. "Don't just stare," said the bear. "I'm in need of repair!" "Oh," said the boy. "Can I help?" "Come up by the stair," said the bear, and he pointed to a rainbow that was trailing behind the cloud.

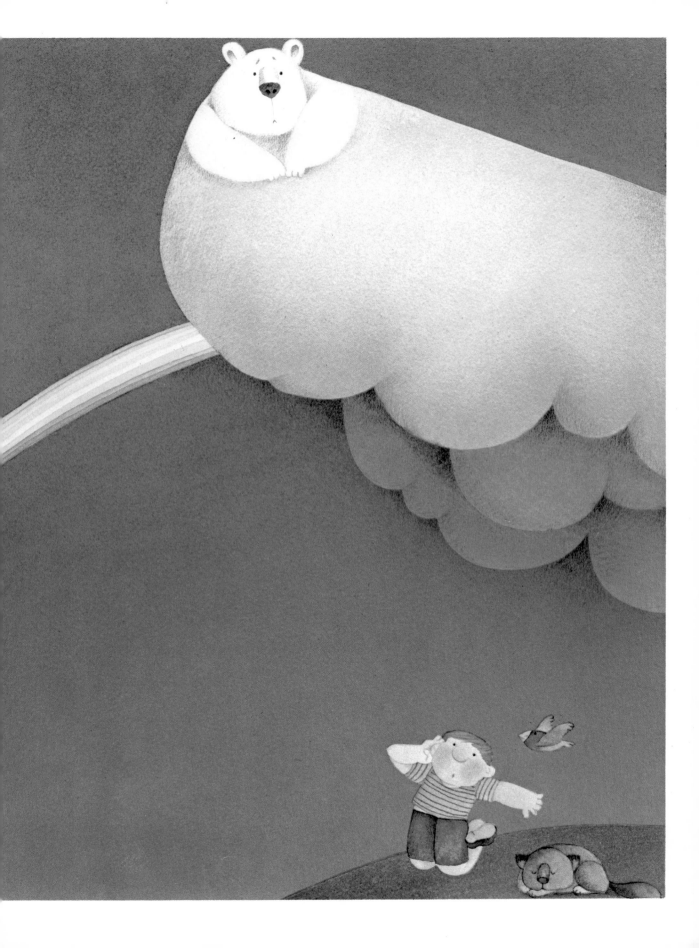

The boy jumped onto the rainbow and found that it was just like an escalator, except that the steps were rainbow-colored: red, orange, yellow, green, blue, indigo and violet.

When he reached the top, the bear was there, white and fluffy, with sky-blue eyes and a tongue as pink as a sunset. On coming closer, the boy could see a tear shining in the corner of the bear's eye. The bear wiped it away with the back of his fuzzy white paw.

"I was in despair," said the bear, "till I saw you there." Then the boy saw that the bear's left foot was caught in a great steel trap.

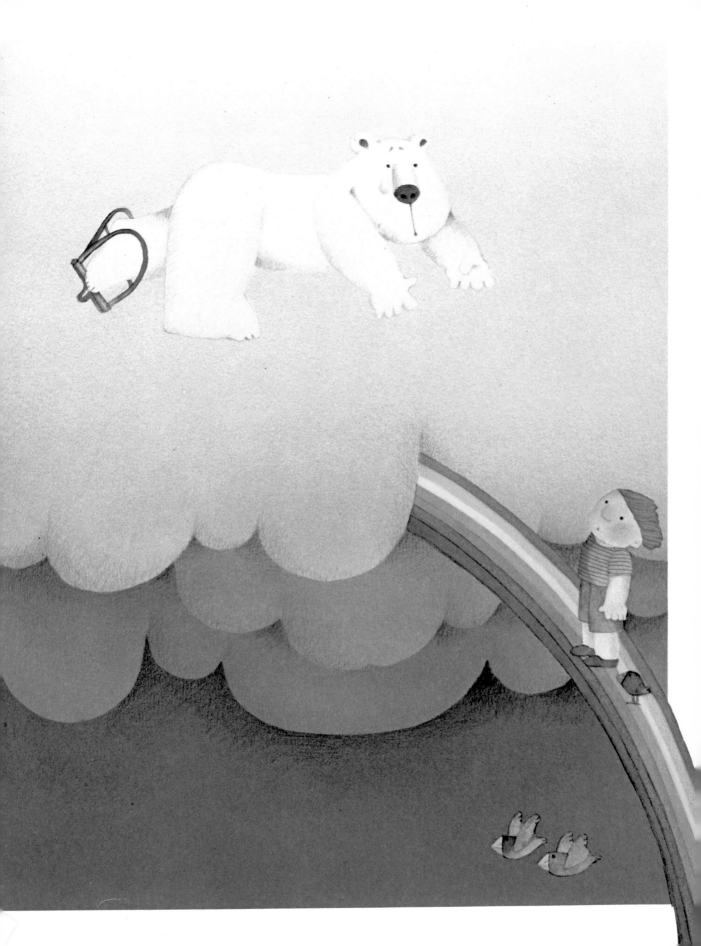

"I am caught in this snare," said the bear in the air.

"Good heavens," said the boy. "That looks nasty!"

"There was no one to care," sniffed the bear in the air.

"Well, I care!" said the boy. "If you lie down, perhaps I could pry it off!"

So the bear lay down and the boy took the trap in both hands and pulled with all his might. Instantly the bear jerked his leg out of the snare and gave such a growl that the boy dropped the trap and nearly fell off the edge of the cloud.

The bear sat down in front of his cave and looked at his ankle. Foam-rubber stuffing was popping out of the rip in the fabric. The boy came over to have a look.

"It's a rather large tear," said the bear in the air. "Have you a needle and thread?" asked the boy. "I'm not awfully good at sewing things, but I can try."
"Somewhere in my lair," said the bear, with a wave of his paw.

The boy walked into the cave and waited for his eyes to grow accustomed to the dark. It was a very messy cave. The bed was rumpled. The sink was full of pots and pans, and a number of jars stood on a shelf, some with lids, some without.

On the same shelf was a box labeled "Patches." That looked helpful, so the boy picked it up and took it outside.

"I found this. Will it do?" he said. The bear
nodded grimly.
"It's a three-corner tear. Find a patch that is
square."

The boy searched in the box until he found a
square patch that was just the right size. Then he
picked a spool of thread and a needle out of the
box.

The boy took the bear's ankle gently in his hands
and said, "This may hurt." But stitches were as
nothing to the bear who, after all, had seams
running up and down both sides of him. The boy
did a neat row of stitches all around the patch and
finished with a firm knot.

The bear looked at the boy's handiwork and nodded.

"You've a flair for repair," said the bear in the air.

"Thank you," said the boy, blushing faintly.

The bear looked at him closely. Then, suddenly, he said, "Would you care to share my lair in the air?"

"What?" said the boy, astonished at the offer.

"We'd make a great pair," said the bear in the air.

"Do you mean it?" asked the boy.

"Of course," said the bear. "There's room to spare."

"We could be friends," said the boy. The bear nodded.

"And you'd be right there if I needed repair."

"It's a deal," said the boy.

"And it's fair," said the bear.

So they shook hands and the bear showed the boy
all over the cloud. The best part was the
observation deck at the back, where they could
lean out and look at the countryside passing
below. It was a wonderful view.

"Do you see that rabbit looking at us?" exclaimed
the boy.
"That's a hare," said the bear.
"And that beautiful horse by the fence?" said the
boy.
"That's a mare," said the bear.
"Pardon me," said the boy, "but do you always
talk like that?"
"Do you care?" said the bear.
"Well. . ." said the boy, because it was beginning
to annoy him just a tiny bit. Then he looked at
the bear out of the corner of his eye and saw that
the bear looked very upset, so he had to say,
"No, of course not."

Then, to change the subject, the boy said,
"Listen, do you hear anything?"
The bear lifted his head and turned his big round
ears from side to side. "A trumpet's blare?"
asked the bear.
"Right!" said the boy. "Music! It must be a
circus."
"Or a fair," said the bear.
"There you go again," said the boy. This time he
really was annoyed. "Why do you always talk in
rhyme?"
"That's my affair," said the bear.

"And it's always the same rhyme," said the boy,
stamping his foot.

"You're like a stuck record."

"How unfair to compare," said the bear.

"I can't stand it!" shouted the boy.

"Too much to bear?" asked the bear.

"Please," said the boy, "try to say something else,
anything—even nonsense will do."

The bear shrugged his shoulders and said, "Ring-
a-ding-a-dare."

"No, no, no," said the boy. "We'll have to think
of something else."

The boy bit his lower lip and thought very hard. He looked at the bear and then thought some more. At last he had an idea. "Maybe it's like hiccups," he said. "Maybe we could scare you out of it."

"My kind doesn't scare," said the bear.

"My temper will flare!" shouted the boy. Then he realized what he had said and clapped his hand over his mouth.

"Now you've got me doing it," the boy mumbled from behind his fingers.

"Don't despair," said the bear, very calmly.

"Why must you do that?" asked the boy.

The bear pulled himself up to his full height and cleared his throat. He folded his paws over his stomach in a solemn way and bowed his head.

"I am heir," said the bear, "to a problem that's rare." He swung his head from side to side in an unhappy way.

"You mean," said the boy, "that your whole family talks this way?"

"It's a habit we share," said the bear, nodding his great round head.

The boy nibbled on his lower lip. "Have you ever tried talking any other way?" he asked.

"I'd just stare," said the bear.

"Nonsense," said the boy. "Please try."

"My name's Alistair," said the bear, politely.

"How do you do?" said the boy. "My name's Mordecai. You could try that for a start. Go on— try. Try to say Mordecai."

"I wouldn't dare!" said the bear.
"But you can!" said the boy. "Just try—
Mordecai."

The bear looked unhappy at the idea, but he
tried. He put his lips together in a firm line.
"Mmmm," he said. "Mmmm."
"Try again," said the boy. "Come on, try!
'Mordecai!' "

"Mmmm," said the bear, gritting his teeth.
"Mmmm." The boy jumped up and down.
"Come on," he yelled. "That's the start! Now:
'Mordecai!'" The boy jumped high in the air. So
the bear jumped too, but he landed on his sore
paw.
"Oh, be careful!" said the boy. The bear hopped
around on one foot—the good one—and howled
softly to himself.
"You see how I fare," he said.
"I'm terribly sorry," said the boy.
"Please," said the bear, "would you bring me a
chair?"
"Of course," said the boy.

The chair was a big bulgy one and it was very
heavy. As the boy came back, pushing and
shoving the chair, he heard the bear muttering to
himself. It sounded like a rumble of thunder.
"Mmmm. Rrrr," muttered the bear in a private
sort of way.

The boy stood quietly so as not to disturb the
bear, who was concentrating very hard.
"Mmmmm. . . . rrr . . . ddd. . ." rumbled the
bear.

Then he threw back his head and pointed his muzzle to the sky. He opened his mouth once or twice, but nothing came out until finally a sound exploded from the bear like a thunderclap. "Mordecai!" roared the bear. "Mordecai! Mordecai!"

There was a streak of lightning as he said the name and a great rush of wind. Rain came pelting down out of the sky. But the boy and the bear were so happy that they danced in the rain, slipping and sliding on the wet cloud.

"Mordecai," said the bear, "we will ride through the sky, just we two, you and I, and we'll eat. . ." The bear had to stop to search for the right word. "Apple pie!" said the boy, dancing right up on the observation deck and waving both arms over his head in the delicious wet rain that streamed down from the sky.

He tilted back his head and opened his mouth to let the raindrops in. Not watching where he was going, he went right on dancing, and with one final fling, flung himself right off the cloud. "Mordecai!" cried the bear, as he saw the boy disappear over the edge of the cloud. "Mordecai!"

Fortunately, it was raining in sheets and the boy tumbled onto one as he fell, sliding safely down to the ground, where he landed with a bump.

He was wet. It was raining. And very
faintly, far in the distance, he thought
he heard someone call his name.

Without knowing why,
he looked up at the sky,
and there, riding high,
was the bear in the air,
who waved a goodbye
to his friend, Mordecai.

**Colophon**
Designed by Barbara Holdridge
Composed by Typesetters, Inc., Baltimore, Maryland
in Times Roman, with display lines in Torino/Flair
Printed by Blackie and Son Ltd., Great Britain
Bound by Delmar Printing Company, Charlotte, North Carolina